D0064604

© 2021 Viacom International Inc. All rights reserved. Published in the United States by Random House Children's Books, a division of Penguin Random House LLC, 1745 Broadway, New York, NY 10019, and in Canada by Penguin Random House Canada Limited, Toronto. Random House and the colophon are registered trademarks of Penguin Random House LLC. Nickelodeon, SpongeBob SquarePants, and all related titles, logos, and characters are trademarks of Viacom International Inc.

created by

Stephen Hillenburg

ISBN 978-0-593-37404-7 (trade)

rhcbooks.com

Printed in the United States of America

10 9 8 7 6 5 4 3 2 1

nickelodeon

JOKE BOOK

By David Lewman

Random House   New York

What did Gary pack before he went to Kamp Koral?

His *sluggage.*

What did SpongeBob keep asking his parents on the way to Kamp Koral?

"Are we *square* yet?

Where do undersea dwellers go when school's out?

Summer *damp.*

Where do shrimp go when school's out?

Summer *scampi.*

Where do sleepy kids go when school's out?

Slumber camp.

Where do squids go when school's out?

Sucker camp.

What's the best sleepaway camp for singers?

Kamp *Choral*.

Why did Sandy make friends with SpongeBob and Patrick right away?

Squirrels love nuts!

What's the best sleepaway camp for kids who like to argue?

Kamp *Quarrel.*

Where do brooms go in the summer?

Sweepaway camp.

Why did the bucket go to summer camp?

To make new *pails*.

Why do pirates go to summer camp?

To get some fresh *airrr.*

Where do frogs go in the summer?

Leapaway camp.

Where do bugs go in the summer?

Creepaway camp.

Why did Gary go away for the summer?

He wanted to be a *campurr*.

Why did the palm tree go to summer camp?

To make new *fronds*.

What happened to the two insects at summer camp?

They became best *bugs.*

What has long fangs, wears a big cape, and sleeps all day in his cabin?

A *campire.*

Where did the ghost learn about camping?

From the *Ghoul* Scouts.

Why did the bubble camper cry on the first day?

He was *foamsick*.

What's the best sleepaway camp for dentists?

Kamp *Oral*.

What do goofy campers wear?

Loonyforms.

What's Kamp Director Krabs' favorite chore?

Taking out the *cash*.

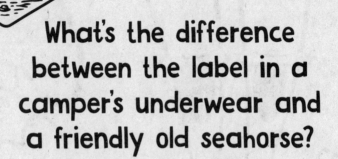

What's the difference between the label in a camper's underwear and a friendly old seahorse?

One's a name tag and
the other's a tame nag.

Why can't seahorses at Kamp Koral agree on new rules?

They always vote *"neigh."*

What did the clown sew into his summer camp clothing?

Name *gags*.

What do ducks like best about summer camp?

The *quacktivities*.

Why did the chicken cross the zip line?

To get to the other *glide*.

What do jellyfish like best about summer camp?

Riding on the *zap* line.

What game did the witch challenge the campers to?

Tug-of-*wart*.

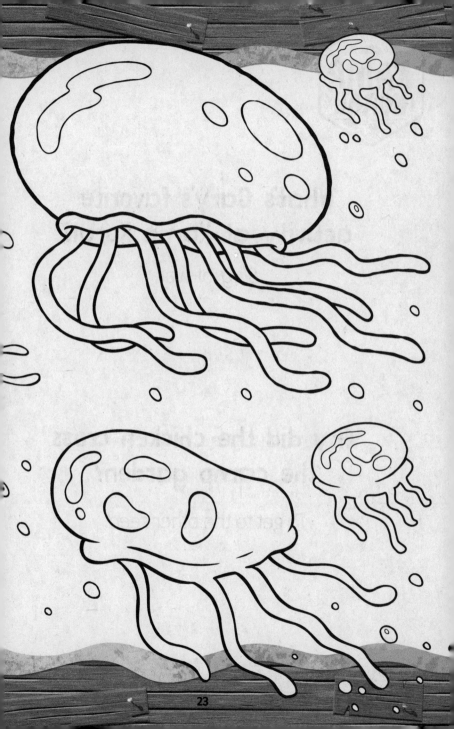

What's Gary's favorite activity at Kamp Koral?

Slug-of-war.

Why did the chicken cross the camp garden?

To get to the other *seed*.

Why did the vampire fly to the baseball field?

It was his turn at *bat*.

What baseball position does Kamp Director Krabs play?

Pinch hitter.

What has strings, a handle, and a powerful engine?

A tennis *rocket*.

What's Patrick's favorite Olympic event?

The *snack* race.

What's the best game to play next to Lake Yuckymuck?

Ickball.

Why did Patrick bring ribbon to the archery range?

He'd heard he needed a *bow*.

What did the clumsy camper learn with a bow and arrows?

Ouchery.

What game do pirates like to play at camp?

Capture the *Swag*.

Why did Patrick bring a sketch pad to the archery range?

He'd heard he was going to *draw* a bow.

What camp activity do sea snakes like best?

Fang gliding.

How did Patrick do with his bow?

He shot a lot of *errors*.

What did the archer wear to the fancy party?

A *bow* tie.

Why did the witch go to Kamp Koral?

For the team *warts*.

What camp sport do worms like best?

Crawlyball.

Why did the rock hound go to Kamp Koral?

For the team *quartz*.

Why did Patrick put a bag over his head for the Kamp Koral Olympics?

He thought he'd entered the sack *face.*

What's it called when campers kick a ball at the bottom of the sea?

Davy Jones's *soccer.*

What's Squidward's favorite Olympic event?

The *snobstacle* course.

Why did Patrick bring a mop to the Kamp Koral Olympics?

He'd heard there was going to be a *swabstacle* course.

Where's the best place to buy water balloons?

At a *sopping* mall.

What do you get when you throw a water balloon at a dish of ice cream?

A banana *splat.*

What's Squidward's favorite Olympic event?

The four-legged race.

Why don't water balloons go to school?

They'd disrupt the class with their *outbursts*.

Which fish gets in the most water balloon fights?

The great *wet* shark.

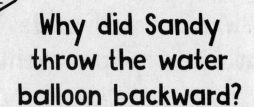

Why did Sandy throw the water balloon backward?

She wanted to try reverse *soakology*.

What do pirates like to toss at each other?

Water *doubloons*.

Which camp activity do ghosts like best?

The scavenger *haunt*.

Patrick:

Can you catch a jellyfish with a woodwind?

SpongeBob:

Sure, if it's a *clarinet*.

Patrick:

Can you catch a jellyfish with a horn?

SpongeBob:

Sure, if it's a *cornet*.

Patrick:

Can you catch a jellyfish with a puppet?

SpongeBob:

Sure, if it's a *marionette*.

Patrick:

Can you catch a jellyfish with your hair?

SpongeBob:

Sure, if you're a *brunette*.

Patrick:

Can you catch a jellyfish with your hands?

SpongeBob:

Sure, but you'll get stung.

What's it called when Kamp Koral campers catch skunks in nets?

Smellyfishing.

What's it called when Kamp Koral campers catch lunch meat in nets?

Delifishing.

What's it called when Kamp Koral campers catch Patrick in a net?

Bellyfishing.

Why did Patrick dig a hole under the cabin?

He'd heard they were going to make friendship *basements*.

Which movie star loves making camp crafts?

Lanyard DiCaprio.

Which time zone is Kamp Koral in?

Central *Lanyard* Time.

SpongeBob:
Knock, knock.

Sandy:
Who's there?

SpongeBob:
Beach.

Sandy:
Beach who?

SpongeBob:
***Beach* you to
Lake Yuckymuck!**

What do math lovers do on rainy days at camp?

Arts and *graphs*.

Why is Plankton so good at camp projects?

He's *crafty*.

Why did Plankton punch the sand?

He wanted to *hit* the beach.

Why did SpongeBob dig a moat around his friend at the beach?

He wanted to build a *Sandycastle*.

Who got to the beach first, the big wave or the little wave?

In the end, they were *tide*.

SpongeBob:
Knock, knock.

Patrick:
Who's there?

SpongeBob:
Canoe.

Patrick:
Canoe who?

SpongeBob:
Canoe paddle harder? We're going in circles.

What's big and blue and feels good on a sunburn?

The Pacific *Lotion.*

What does SpongeBob use to write home from the beach?

Sandpaper.

What do elephants wear in Lake Yuckymuck?

Their swimming *trunks.*

Which oar is no good for rowing a boat?

A *dinosaur.*

What do you call it when two oars fall in love?

True *rowmance.*

KAMP KORAL

What does Gary like to do
on Lake Yuckymuck?

Go *snailing.*

How do campers choose
who has to use the oars?

Eeny, meeny, miny, *row.*

Why was Patrick sad at the end of his rowing lesson?

He missed the boat.

What do you get when you cross the bottom of a tree with a dock on the lake?

Root *pier.*

Why did Patrick throw the can of brown soda into Lake Yuckymuck?

He wanted to make a root beer *float*.

What do you call two spuds in a canoe?

Splashed potatoes.

Why is Lake Yuckymuck the best place to get sick?

There's always a *dock*.

What did Sandy invent to make her boat go?

A *rowbot*.

Why did Patrick chase mantas and stingers at the beach?

He'd heard he was supposed to catch some *rays*.

What do math lovers do at the beach?

Sumbathe.

How do parrots keep from getting burned on the beach?

Lots of *sunsquawk.*

What do you call an insult from a star?

A *sunburn*.

When is a book like a sunburned camper?

When it's been *read*.

What do you call a sunburned Kamp Director?

Blister Krabs.

Squidward:
Knock, knock.

SpongeBob:
Who's there?

Squidward:
Romeo.

SpongeBob:
Romeo who?

Squidward:
Row me over to the other side of Lake Yuckymuck, and make it snappy!

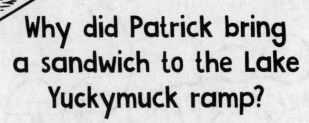

Why did Patrick bring a sandwich to the Lake Yuckymuck ramp?

He'd heard there was going to be a boat *lunch*.

Why did Patrick bring a pumpkin to Lake Yuckymuck?

He wanted to try *paddlegourding*.

What's it called when campers blab while paddling?

Kayakking.

What has long hair, sharp horns, and paddles?

A *kayyak!*

Why does SpongeBob never take more than two hikes in a day?

Three *hikes* and you're out!

Sunburned SpongeBob:
Knock, knock.

Patrick:
Who's there?

Sunburned SpongeBob:
I'm ready!

Patrick:
I'm ready who?

Sunburned SpongeBob:
**I'm *red even* though
I wore sunblock!**

Why didn't SpongeBob want to talk about his feet after the long hike?

They were a *sore* subject.

What's the best kind of pen when you're lost in the desert?

A *fountain* pen.

What's the difference between a squeeze from a rabbit and one from a bee?

One's a bunny hug and the other's a honey bug.

Why did the traveling bug land on the camper?

He wanted to stop for a quick *bite*.

How did the doctor invent a cure for poison kelp?

He started from *scratch*.

Why did Patrick hike through the poison kelp?

He was *itching* to go.

Why did the camper keep getting bugbites?

He really couldn't *spray*.

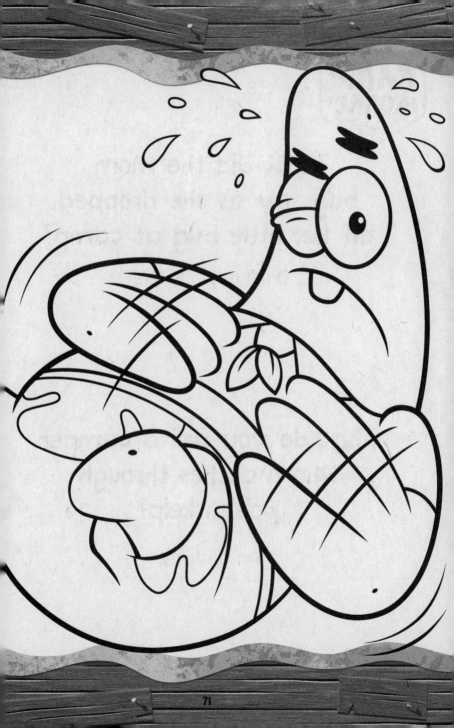

KAMP KORAL

What did the mom bug say as she dropped off her little bug at camp?

"Don't forget to *bite*!"

What do you call a camper who marches through poison kelp?

An *itchhiker.*

When are campers like lottery tickets?

When they're *scratchers*.

What does Sandy always bring on a hike?

Her *furst* aid kit.

Where did the sloppy camper go hiking?

The *wildermess*.

Why did Patrick go hiking without a map?

Squidward told him to get *lost*.

Where did the clumsy camper go hiking?

The Great *Ouchdoors*.

Which reptile is the best at reading trail maps?

The *navigator.*

What should campers do when they run out of seaweed?

Send for *kelp.*

On a hiking trail, what comes after the forest?

The *five-est*.

Why did Patrick go hiking with a bunch of dogfish?

He wanted to take a walk in the *woofs*.

Why did Patrick put glue on his feet before he went hiking?

Squidward told him to *stick* to the trail.

What do Kamp Koral employees do when Mr. Krabs won't give them a raise?

Go on *hike.*

What's the difference between taking a snack on a hike and juggling envelopes?

One's trail mix and the other's mail tricks.

KAMP KORAL

What do you call it when a hiker says "I don't need a map"?

Famous *lost* words.

What happened to Patrick when he drank too much soda and marched up Porpoise Peak?

He got a bad case of the *hikeups.*

Why did Patrick pretend to go on the trail?

He thought Squidward told him to *fake* a hike.

What do baseball players always bring on a hike?

Trail *mitts.*

Who's in charge of the kelp forest?

The commander in *leaf.*

SpongeBob:
Knock, knock.

Patrick:
Who's there?

SpongeBob:
Nate.

Patrick:
Nate who?

SpongeBob:
***Nate-ure* trails are the best! Let's go!**

Why do quarterbacks make the best campers?

They're always ready to take a *hike*.

Why couldn't the chasm near Kamp Koral ever sit down?

It was *bottomless*.

What's Squidward's favorite kind of chasm?

Sarcasm.

What do spiders eat at picnics?

Corn on the *cobweb.*

What snack goes best with an underwater lunch?

Potato *drips.*

When is food like Plankton?

When it goes *bad*.

What's the difference between a wiener and someone who grabs all the spots?

One's a hot dog and the other's a dot hog.

What's green and comes on a bun?

A *hambooger.*

Why did Patrick dive into Plankton's pot?

He wanted to join the *grub.*

Why did Patrick bring a flyswatter to Kamp Koral's performance night?

He'd heard there was going to be a talent *shoo.*

Why did the camper bring bread to the talent show?

She wanted to break into *dough* business.

Why did Plankton enter Kamp Koral's talent night?

He wanted to *steal* the show.

Why did Sandy visit the desert before talent night?

She'd heard *cactus* makes perfect.

Why did Patrick bring a baseball to talent night?

He'd heard it was important
to stay on *pitch*.

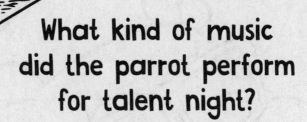

What kind of music did the parrot perform for talent night?

Squawk 'n' roll.

Why did Patrick build a campfire before talent night?

He'd heard it was important to *warm* up.

Why don't eggs sing high notes?

They always *crack.*

Why aren't flounders good singers?

They're always *flat.*

Why aren't swordfish good singers?

They're always *sharp.*

Was the log entertaining at the wienie roast?

Yeah, he was *on fire*!

Why did Patrick throw candy on the burning log?

He wanted to make a *bonbon* fire.

What do you use to fix a broken chimney?

A fire *drill*.

How is Patrick on a hike like a campfire in the rain?

They're both hard to get started.

How can you tell when a campfire is sick?

It doesn't feel so *hot.*

How did the branch avoid the campfire?

He took a *stick* day.

Are hot dogs brave?

No, they're *wienies.*

What happened to the log that wouldn't burn?

It finally met its *match*.

What kind of match is no good for starting a fire?

A tennis *match*.

What do sea stars like to do around the campfire?

Have a *cling*-along.

What do jellyfish like to do around the campfire?

Have a *sting*-along.

Which pirate loves warbling around a campfire?

Sing-*Along* John Silver.

How did the log feel about being in a campfire?

Burned up.

What do campfires eat for breakfast?

Shredded *heat.*

How did Patrick choose
which hot dog to roast?

Wienie, meeny, miny, mo.

What kind of branch
never burns?

The *branch* of a river.

What did the robber say when he held a branch over his head?

"This is a *stickup*!"

How is a camper who gathers firewood like a banker?

She's a *branch* manager.

What do termites eat for breakfast?

Branch flakes.

What do frogs roast over campfires?

Hop dogs.

What do campers use to burn logs when they don't have matches?

Fireflies.

If Squidward were a branch, what kind would he be?

A *stick*-in-the-mud.

What do owls roast over campfires?

Hoot dogs.

What do boogers roast over campfires?

Snot dogs.

Why are campers never satisfied?

Because they always want *s'mores.*

What do mushrooms make around the campfire?

S'pores.

What do camping bugs make on windshields?

S'mears.

What do soldiers use to make s'mores?

Marchmallows.

KAMP KORAL

Sandy:
What do cows like to make over a campfire?

Patrick:
What?

Sandy:
S'moo-ers!

Patrick:
What's a cow?

What do dry cleaners use to make s'mores?

Starchmallows.

What do frogs use to make s'mores?

Marshmallows, chocolate bars, and graham *croakers.*

What do oysters use to make s'mores?

Marshmallows, chocolate bars, and *clam* crackers.

What do parrots use to make s'mores?

Marshmallows, graham crackers, and *squawklate* bars.

What do electric eels use to make s'mores?

Marshmallows, graham crackers, and *shocklate* bars.

What does Mrs. Puff use to make s'mores?

Marshmallows, graham crackers, and *chalklate* bars.

What does Patrick make by the campfire late at night?

S'nores.

What kind of fire is safe for a baby camper?

A *pacifier.*

What do alligators use to make s'mores?

Marshmallows, graham crackers, and *croclate* bars.

Why did Patrick raise a glass to the marshmallow?

He'd heard he was supposed to *toast* it.

What kind of stick makes the worst kindling?

Lipstick.

What kind of fire should you never use to roast hot dogs?

A sapphire.

What did SpongeBob tell Patrick when he was searching for the campfire?

"You're getting *warmer*!"

What do trees get when they hear ghost stories?

Goose *stumps*.

What do sheep campers tell around the campfire?

Goat stories.

What's the difference between a trim and a nurse's cabin?

One's a haircut and the other's a care hut.

How do fast-food cooks relax in summer?

They sit around the *campfryer*.

What do you call a wagon full of camp beds?

A load of *bunk*.

What do waves tell around the campfire?

Coast stories.

What does SpongeBob like to do around the campfire at night?

Tell *Gary* stories.

What kind of music do campers play in their beds?

Bunk rock.

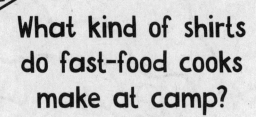

What kind of shirts do fast-food cooks make at camp?

Fry-dyed.

Why did Patrick wear a turtleneck on the last day of camp?

He'd heard they were having a *collar* war.

What kind of cot is the worst to sleep on?

An *apricot.*